Christmas 2001

Mrs. Thomschke:

We thought you'd enjoy this little book as much as we did.

your gentle and kind heart make you a true blessing to our little ones at St. Patrick's School.

May God bless you always,

Patty, Craig &
Kevin
Collie

International Standard Book Number 0-942865-22-7

Manufactured in the United States of America

100 Minnesota Avenue
Le Sueur, MN 56058

remember the manger...

Story by Kimberly Rinehart

Illustrations by Georgia Rettmer

remember the manger

remember the wisemen

who came from afar.

remember the baby
so tiny and new

God's great gift of love
that was given for you.

remember the stable
        so humble and bare

remember the hope
   that was filling the air.

remember the mother
whose heart sang for joy

and the gentle
   new father
who cradled his boy.

remember the angels
who watched from above

and sheltered the babe
in the wings
of their love.

remember the shepherds
who knelt and adored

the tiny new king
who was surely their Lord.

remember the creatures
who all gathered 'round

and welcomed the child
without making a sound.

remember
the cold
lonely
darkness
that night

that was changed   for all time